D0574694

Garbage Dog

Written by Robbie Wilkinson
Illustrated by Eleni Kalorkoti

This book was edited and designed by gestalten.

Typeface: Objektiv Mk1 by Dalton Maag

Printed by Grafisches Centrum Cuno GmbH & Co.KG, Calbe (Saale)
Made in Germany

Published by Little Gestalten, Berlin 2019
ISBN 978-3-89955-832-6

Eleni Kalorkoti—With thanks and love to Lizzy and Jon.
Robbie Wilkinson—For Frank, Dora and Rocky. And special thanks to
Monica Melinsky and Imogen Grasby.

For more information, and to order books, please visit www.little.gestalten.com.

Bibliographic information published by the Deutsche Nationalbibliothek.
The Deutsche Nationalbibliothek lists this publication in the Deutsche Nationalbibliografie;
detailed bibliographic data are available online at www.dnb.de.

This book was printed on paper certified according to the standards of the FSC®.

Garbage Dog

Eleni Kalorkoti
Robbie Wilkinson

This is Garbage Dog, he lives in the city.
His home's an old box and it's not very pretty.
It's down a dark alley all scattered with litter,
Behind a café called The Pot-Bellied Critter.

His fur is matted with
Lumps of old sludge,
He hasn't been bathed
So the smell doesn't budge.

At the back of his mind, he remembers an old friend,
With gray hair and wrinkles, whose love didn't end.
He remembers the smell of freshly cooked dinners,
And a bed in the corner of a bright-colored room.
But now from his box, he only sees rats,
Sad skinny strays, and bony old cats.

Each Sunday at noon as food's being grilled,
Baked or boiled and all bellies filled,

Smells float from the door and into his nose.
He shuts his brown eyes and imagines the show.

There's ham and chicken and gravy with peas,
Bright summer cakes and big chunks of cheese.

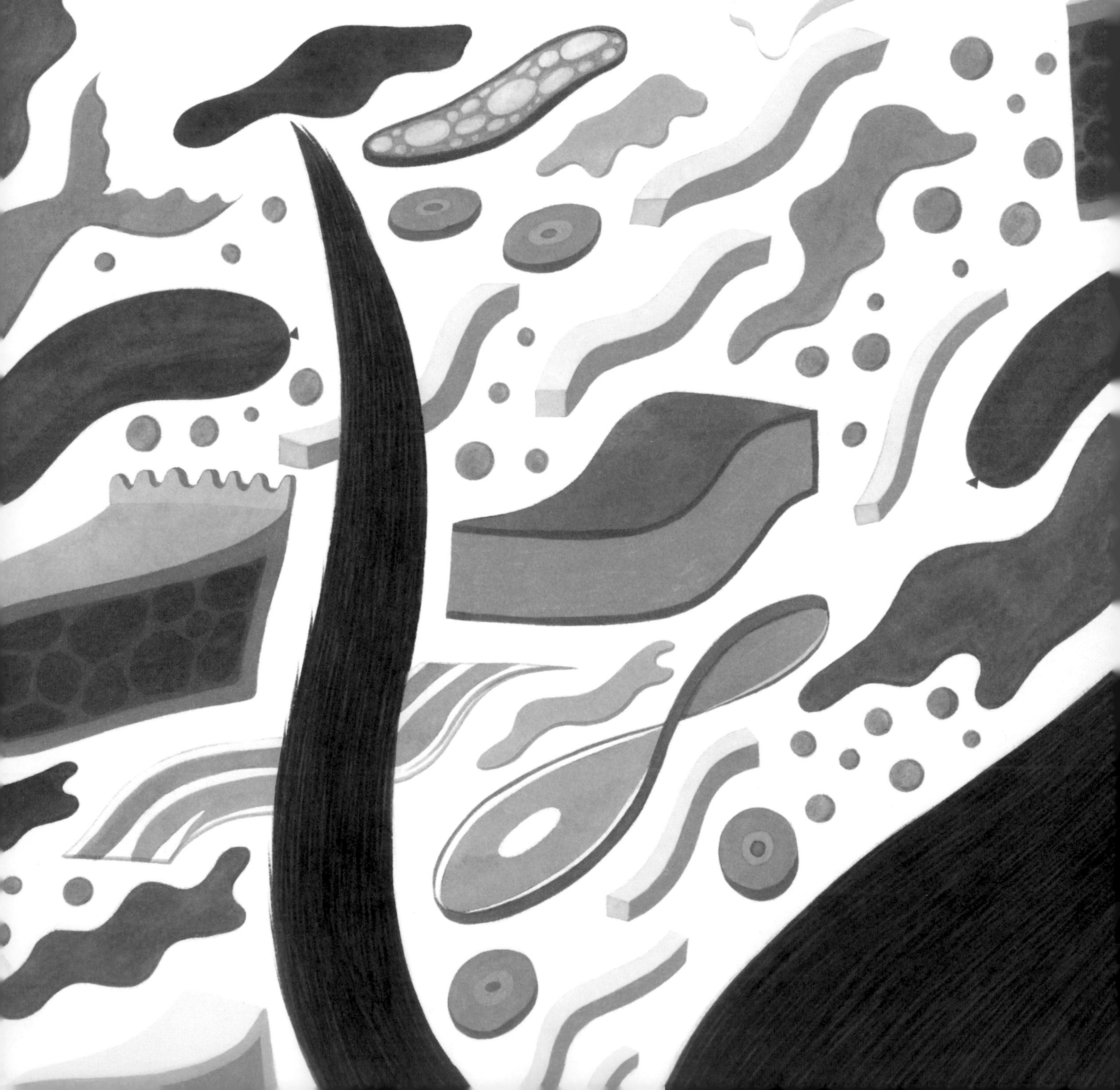

The men from the kitchen watch the back door,
As they munch on their breakfast and pastries galore.
They chuckle at the animals, so hungry and weak,
And titter as they throw what's left in the street.
So Garbage Dog waits as they take out the trash,
Hoping for bin bags that pop in a flash...

Now he has to be fast, he's not on his own
There's a mean cat called Jerry and a big dog called Joan.

Hurt and abandoned when their owners left town,
They've been here a long time and they wear a mean frown.

Jerry moves quickly and gets the prime cut.
He's first on the scene and eats it all up.
Joan is so big she'll get all the rest,
Once she is done there are only scraps left.

But back in his box Garbage Dog opens his paw,
And scatters some crumbs down onto the floor.
He smiles at the mice, now sat by his feet,
"Don't worry, little friends...here's something to eat"

The days pass by and more strangers arrive,
With the hope of a bed, or a big meal outside.
Dogs and cats, so many new faces,
Searching for food in so many places.

It’s getting packed in the alley, there isn’t much spare
They all dash for the scraps without manners or care
You have to be quick, mean-spirited and tough,
There are too many mouths and never enough.

One cold night as he dreams of fresh bread,
Joan creeps up to his box and fills him with dread.
She pushes and squeezes into his house.
She sits on his bed and eats a dead mouse.

Jerry watches quietly from up on the stairs,
He laughs at the dog, who is soaking and scared.

When Jerry gets closer he lashes out a claw,
And jabs it down hard on a shivering wet paw.
"Why are you here? You smell like a bog!
There's no space for you, you foul Garbage Dog!"

The city is scary and people are mean,
So Garbage Dog runs trying not to be seen.

Loud roaring cars and big flashing lights,
Shouting and smashing all through the night.

As a truck lunges down
a bumpy wet track,
There's a poor speckled mouse
that's about to get whacked.

He jumps over to help it away from the danger,
The mouse shouts back, "Why thank you, kind stranger!"

For weeks he sleeps under benches and boxes,
Meeting friendly pigeons and red-tailed foxes.
Whenever he sees another creature in need,
He does what he can, regardless the breed.

On days when it rains, he helps mice find cover,
He always shares snacks that he might discover.

No matter the weather, no matter his mood,
He tells himself quietly, "Be kind and be good."

One crisp winter's morning, he is hungry and cold,
When someone appears with a handful of food.

He's put in a cage and feels a bit scared,
But the woman is kind and speaks like she cares.

She cleans him and brushes him and pats his head,
He wags his small tail at the treats he's fed.

He is welcomed with tickles, with hugs and with kisses,
They like to play ball, and it's all that he wishes.
He's given a collar with a shiny gold pin,
The letters spell "Buddy", a name just for him.

BUDDY

Each Sunday at noon as food's being grilled,
Baked or boiled and all bellies filled,

Smells float from the kitchen and into his nose
His family call out, "It's dinner time soon!"